A TIGER CALLED THOMAS

Charlotte Zolotow

A TIGER CALLED THOMAS

pictures by Catherine Stock

Lothrop, Lee & Shepard Books   **New York**

Second Edition 1 2 3 4 5 6 7 8 9 10

Library of Congress Cataloging in Publication Data
Zolotow, Charlotte. A tiger called Thomas.
Summary: New to the neighborhood, Thomas is shy about making friends until he wears a
tiger suit on Halloween. [1. Moving, Household—Fiction. 2. Friendship—Fiction.
3. Halloween—Fiction.] I. Stock, Catherine, ill. II. Title.
PZ7.Z77Ti 1988 [E] 86-20878
ISBN 0-688-06696-8 ISBN 0-688-06697-6 (lib. bdg.)

To Augusta McCarthy, once again
—c.z.

For Allyn
—c.s.

Once there was a little boy named Thomas.

He had brown eyes and brown hair and was quite nice.

But when he and his family moved to a new house on a new street, he took it into his head that the new people might not like him.

So he never went off his new porch.

"Why don't you play with that little girl Marie?" his mother asked him.

"Maybe she wouldn't like me," Thomas said.

"Of course she'd like you," his mother said. "Why shouldn't she?"

But Thomas didn't answer.

"Why don't you visit the lady with the black cat down the street?" his mother asked.

"They might not like me," Thomas said.

"Of course they'd like you. Why shouldn't they like you?" said his mother.

But Thomas didn't go.

"That tall boy named Gerald looks lonely," his mother said.

"I don't think he'd like me," said Thomas.

"Of course he'd like you," said Thomas's mother. "Why shouldn't he like you? Everybody likes you."

But Thomas wouldn't leave his new porch.

He just sat there and watched when Marie played
hopscotch.

He sat there and watched the old woman's cat as it prowled through the grass and shrubs.

He sat there and watched when Gerald walked past the house, and thought how tall he was.

"Oh, Thomas," said his mother, "everyone will like you. Why don't you go play?"

But Thomas shook his head and just sat on the new porch...watching.

The lady in the house across the street was always out in her garden, watering the plants, raking the leaves, sweeping the sidewalk, picking her flowers. And all the while Thomas sat on his new porch and watched.

He watched the old man who came up the street with his big black poodle three times a day.

The poodle always looked over its shoulder at Thomas, and its tail stood up like a small palm tree and wagged from side to side.

But Thomas just sat on his porch and watched them
pass.

He watched the sparrows and the grackles and the blue
jays in the trees.

He watched the black cat look up at the sparrows and
grackles and blue jays.

But he never went off the porch to play.

At Halloween his mother came home with a tiger outfit for him.

"Try this on," she said.

He put on the orange-and-black-striped suit with its quilted tail.

He put on the mask with its long whiskers.

"How do I look?" he asked his mother.

"Exactly like a tiger," she said.

Thomas looked in the mirror and his mother was right.

"No one will know who I am when I go trick or treating," he said.

There was a large orange moon in the sky, and it was already getting dark when Thomas went out. The branches of the trees hardly showed, except where they laced across the moon.

He crossed the street to the house of the lady who was always outside. The chrysanthemums were still blooming in front of her house.

"Trick or treat," Thomas called when she came to the door.
"Well, hello!" the lady said. She dropped a package of
orange candies into his bag. "Happy Halloween."

"Thank you," answered the tiger.
"You're welcome, Thomas," the lady said, closing the door.
Under his mask Thomas flushed.
That's odd, he thought. She called the tiger Thomas.

At the next house he rang the bell.

"Trick or treat," he called.

Marie's mother opened the door. She had candy apples for the treat.

"Oh, thank you," the tiger said, for he especially liked candy apples.

"You're welcome," said Marie's mother. "Marie is a witch tonight. Maybe you'll pass her, but anyway come play hopscotch here tomorrow, Thomas."

"Thank you," Thomas said again.

But when the door closed, he reached up to feel his mask. It was still on, covering his whole face.

That's odd, he thought. She knew who I was too.

He passed a tall ghost going up the stairs as he went down. He couldn't see his face, but there was something very familiar about his figure.

"Hi, Thomas," said the ghost. "Want to play horseshoes tomorrow? I got a new set."

"Sure," said Thomas. For the ghost was Gerald. He could tell by his height.

He went on to the old man's house.

The black poodle threw back his head and barked wildly when he saw the tiger at the door. But when he sniffed at the tiger's feet and sniffed at the tiger's quilted tail, he suddenly put up his own palm-tree one and wagged it hard.

"Trick or treat," the tiger said.

The old man dropped a big pumpkin cookie into the bag. "Fresh made, Thomas," he said. "Best thing for tigers," he added.

He called the tiger Thomas too, thought Thomas.

Now he rang the bell at the house of the lady and the black cat.

"Trick or treat," he called.

"Come in, come in," the little old woman said. Her black cat looked curiously at the tiger, and the tiger reached out to stroke the cat's black slippery fur.

"He loves that." The little old lady laughed. "Come play with him again, Thomas," she said. "He gets lonely."

"So do I," said Thomas.

She knew too, he thought to himself as he turned toward home.

The orange moon was a little higher in the sky. The sky was a little blacker than before. He couldn't see any of the branches against it now.

A group of ghosts and goblins were coming down the steps of the lady across the street. And a solitary but familiar-looking witch with her broom under her arm passed him. He looked at her curiously as he walked slowly up the steps of his front porch. It was Marie.

"Hi, Thomas," called Marie.

He walked upstairs to his own room.

He looked in the mirror at the tiger.

The tiger in the mirror looked back at him, whiskers and all.

"Have a good time?" asked his mother.

"How did they all know who I am?" Thomas asked.

"Did they?" said his mother.

"Yes," Thomas said. "The mask didn't fool them a bit. And they all asked me back."

"I guess they all like you," his mother said.

Thomas looked at her.

Suddenly he felt wonderful.

"Oh, I like them too!" he said, and when he took off the
mask, he was smiling.